E
Rad

DATE DUE 4/12

		SEP 1 2 2012	
JAN 3 0 2012		OCT 0 3 2012	
FEB 1 3 2012		OCT 0 8 2012	
MAR 0 7 2012		NOV 0 2 2012	
MAR 1 7 2012	NOV 2 6 2012		
APR 0 7 2012		DEC 0 3 2012	
APR 2 0 2012	OCT 1 1 2019		
MAY 1 6 2012			
JUN 2 8 2012			
AUG 0 1 2012			
AUG 2 3 2012			

DEMCO 38-296

Where to Sleep

by Kandy Radzinski

To Nette and Willard Hudson—
For your wisdom and caring,
and most of all, love.
     —KANDY

Text Copyright © 2009 Kandy Radzinski
Illustration Copyright © 2009 Kandy Radzinski

Sleeping Bear Press™
310 North Main Street, Suite 300
Chelsea, MI 48118
www.sleepingbearpress.com

© 2009 Sleeping Bear Press is an imprint of Gale, a part of Cengage Learning.

Printed and bound in China.

First Edition

10 9 8 7 6 5 4 3 2 1

Library of Congress Cataloging-in-Publication Data

Radzinski, Kandy.
Where to sleep / written and illustrated by Kandy Radzinski.
   p. cm.
Summary: Rhyming text explores different places a kitten might
sleep, finally settling on a best friend's feet.
ISBN 978-1-58536-436-7
[1. Stories in rhyme. 2. Sleep-Fiction. 3. Cats-PZ8.3.R118Whg 2009
[E]-dc22
2008040788

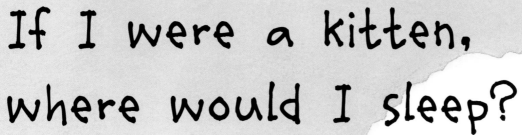

If I were a kitten,
where would I sleep?

I could sleep with
a sweet little cow

but she's not ready
for bed right now.

I could sleep in the vegetable patch

but I'd be looking

for bunnies to catch.

I could sleep with
the chicken flock

but they stay up late
and talk, talk, talk.

I could sleep on the old porch swing

but it's too crowded

with toys and things.

I could sleep in a soft brown shoe

but it's too small,
so that won't do.

I could sleep in
an old armchair

but someone else
already sleeps there.

If I were a kitten, where would I sleep?

All curled up at my best friend's feet!